# The Secret of the Brush

## Sheri Gardner

Halo Publishing International
8000 W Interstate 10, #600
San Antonio, Texas 78230

First Edition, February 2023
Printed in the United States of America
ISBN: 978-1-63765-364-7
Library of Congress Control Number: 2023900364

The information contained within this book is strictly for informational purposes. Unless otherwise indicated, all the names, characters, businesses, places, events and incidents in this book are either the product of the author's imagination or used in a fictitious manner. Any resemblance to actual persons, living or dead, or actual events is purely coincidental.

Halo Publishing International is a self-publishing company that publishes adult fiction and non-fiction, children's literature, self-help, spiritual, and faith-based books. We continually strive to help authors reach their publishing goals and provide many different services that help them do so. We do not publish books that are deemed to be politically, religiously, or socially disrespectful, or books that are sexually provocative, including erotica. Halo reserves the right to refuse publication of any manuscript if it is deemed not to be in line with our principles. Do you have a book idea you would like us to consider publishing? Please visit www.halopublishing.com for more information.

For my believers

Marc, Valerie, and Michael

# Contents

# Prologue

Once upon a time, under a wild Texas sky lived a herd of mysterious, magical horses with wings. These creatures once lived in the southernmost part of the ancient Greek Empire. The most famous winged horse was Pegasus. According to Greek mythology, he became the bearer of thunder and lightning for Zeus. Although he lived in a constellation, Pegasus allowed a single feather of his to fall back down to Earth. This feather had the power to summon him back if needed. The rest of his herd remained on Earth.

Pegasi, the species that remained wild, possessed bodies of small horses with disproportionately-large gossamer wings. Their wings were used to support their weight as they glided over rough terrain, but more often their wings allowed them to rear on their hind legs for a fearsome display to intimidate or frighten an enemy.

Humans did not understand these unique creatures, and as the Greek Empire crumbled, the horses soon were exiled, out of fear, to distant lands. The last of the herd was redirected to Spain by sympathetic Roman centurions who still revered the mysterious animals. The Pegasi lived there in relative obscurity until the flourishing Spanish Empire grew too powerful to share its land with foreign beasts. The Spanish king then issued a decree offering a bounty to anyone presenting the court with a Pegasus hide and wings, for it was rumored that these items still possessed the magical powers bestowed upon them by the Greek gods. The king, however, was sorely disappointed; his scholars could never detect or isolate any unique powers. Soon the Pegasi's dwindling population made it impossible to investigate whether life or virtue contributed to the power of the winged horses.

A young Spanish explorer named Cabeza de Vaca took pity on the plight of the animals being cruelly hunted down and dissected. He smuggled the last few onto his ship traveling westward. When his ship ran aground on an island off what is now the Louisiana/Texas coast, it was apparent he could no longer care for the animals, so he set them free and pursued his search for gold. Out of loyalty to de Vaca, though, it was said the Pegasi followed him on his travels through Texas, protecting him from peril. They lived among the Native Americans until they, too, eventually hunted them for their healing magic.

However, the wild herd soon adapted to their untamed surroundings. They developed a beautiful mottled, light-grey coat, which camouflaged them among the mesquites and dry scrub of the South Texas brush. They became nocturnal, feeding off moonlit vegetation, and then only on the darkest nights. Supposedly they could still seek refuge in the constellation of Pegasus when threatened, but they had no natural predators in the brush. Only a direct shot to the heart was said to cause death, and no one had seen them since the last Native Americans recorded their legends.

Today they are simply regarded as ancient Greek myths or legends of the Native American medicine men. There is no recorded history in Texas of their existence...until possibly now.

## Chapter 1
# Justice

Kanter County is a rather large county that comprises over a thousand square miles of usually flat terrain in South Texas. That is just a little smaller than the state of Rhode Island. The county's land is covered with mesquite, scrub, brush, cacti, chaparral, and grass. The Frio River flows through the northern half of the county before it empties in the southeastern corner into Choke Canyon. The county seat is a little town called Justice.

Native American artifacts demonstrate that humans have lived in this area for approximately 11,000 years. The Coahuiltecan Indians made this area their home, but they were squeezed out by Lipan Apache and other tribes, who were migrating into the area, and by the Spanish who were moving up from the south.

Between the Texas Revolution and the Mexican War, most of what is now Kanter County lay in the disputed area between the Rio Grande and the Frio Rivers. Neither the Republic of Texas nor the Mexican government could establish effective control over this wild strip of contested land, and it became a haven for outlaws and thieves. Nowadays, however, it is better known as the home of the Kanter County Public School Cowboys and Cowgirls, and soon to be the home of Emeralda and Marcus Ruiz, as well.

"It says here that Justice's chief economic activities include wild-game hunting and the processing of natural gas, so what are you going to do, Mom?" asked Em (short for Emeralda) as she read what her mom had printed from an Internet site. Her mother was a pharmacist, and they weren't exactly moving into a mecca for health-care workers.

"We'll worry about that once we are all settled," she answered as if it were the least of her concerns. "I'm sure everything will fall into place. It always does."

That sounded convincing, so Em bought it for the moment. She looked back out of the truck window. The scenery was changing. The tall, lush pecan trees and rich, green grass were quickly shrinking and fading away. The terrain was becoming drier and more open, and they weren't even halfway there.

Emeralda and Marcus's dad was a coach. Not just any coach—a basketball coach. He coached football, too, which was good because, in Texas, football is king. Though Coach Ruiz had coached a lot of football, he lived for basketball season. That is why he took this new job. It was all about basketball, and he would be the head coach of the boys' basketball team. There was no football team.

"What kind of school doesn't have a football team?" Marcus asked.

"A small one," his father replied.

"Will I like it?"

"I hope so. I hope we all like it there."

The conversation was echoing in Em's head as they continued to drive south. She dreaded the thought of making friends all over again. She was not good at making friends and even worse at first impressions. Even though she was courteous and polite, she still came across as bossy. She really wasn't bossy, just brutally honest. If she was right, she wanted to say so, and if she was pushed, she wanted to push back. Fair is fair, right? Apparently not. Evidently fair was not a popular philosophy when trying to make friends. Maybe things would be different in a town called Justice.

Although Em was concerned about making friends, she was still excited about the move. She loved to explore and couldn't wait to see a new part of the state. She'd read there had once been Native Americans in the area, and she was dying to see if she could find any artifacts, like arrowheads, to add to her rock collection. Plus, she was looking forward to living in the country.

Her brother, Marcus, on the other hand, was not looking forward to the move. He loved football and walking the sidelines during his dad's games. He loved their big old house too. It was near their grandparents. His grandfather would take Em and him fishing and let them drive the boat. His grandmother baked all sorts of pies and pastries, and now he wasn't going to be there to enjoy them. Besides, he had a feather collection—blue jays, cardinals, painted buntings, scarlet tanagers, black-birds, crows, mockingbirds, mallards, egrets, sandhill cranes, bobwhites, guineas, peacocks, hummingbirds. What if there were no birds at his new home? His grandfather had told him there would be lots of doves, quails, and turkeys, but those were game birds, and he already had those feathers.

As the truck turned onto Highway 16, Dad said, "Okay, kids, take a good look. This is the last of civilization we'll see for a while."

"This is civilization?" asked Em.

"Well, it is the closest Walmart," he replied.

"Oh my gosh! It is in a field. Are you sure?"

"How much farther?" Marcus chimed in.

"About thirty-five miles, but it's a pretty dull drive," Dad answered.

Dull was right. There was nothing new to see. Old barbed-wire fences guarded fields of dry brush and cacti. The grasses were about knee-high but looked dry and crisp. They were shades of yellow and brown. The brush was already grey, and it was still summer. The cacti were faded green and looked worn, as if the sun had already drained them of all their vibrant colors. No wildlife of any kind could be seen. The sun blazed down, and nothing looked alive. Fence post, fence post, fence post…

"Are we there yet?"

"Not yet."

Occasionally a deer blind broke up the wild pastures, and a few trailers dotted the landscape. For the most part, however, it was more of the same dry, boring scenery. Fence post, fence post, fence post…

"Are we there yet?"

"Almost, see that bridge up ahead? That is the Frio River. Justice is on the other side."

"What bridge?" Marcus asked.

"You mean the wide part of the highway?" asked Em.

"Yeah, that's a bridge, just not very fancy," Dad answered.

"Where's the town?"

"This is it."

## Chapter 2

# A Feather

Two gas stations, a church, a mercantile, a bank, a diner, a courthouse, and a school comprised the town of Justice. The only paved roads were the two highways that crossed it. All the other roads were gravel. Dad turned on the gravel road next to the school, and dust billowed behind the truck. It looked as if the truck were towing a huge white cloud. Several old brick houses lined the road behind the school. They looked as dry and dusty as the road, as if the scorching sun had sucked all the redness out of their bricks. Dad drove to the last one.

The homes were called teacherages, like parsonages for churches; they were houses that the school district rented to teachers. There weren't very many houses in town, certainly not any for sale. Besides a few older homesteads, most were trailers. Since the rest of the county was divided into large ranches, the school district's only solution was to provide homes for new teachers.

Their new home didn't look like much from the out-side. A row of transplanted evergreens lined one side of the driveway, and on the other side, there was about a twenty-foot drop where the school had started building a new all-weather track. There was one tree in the yard. It was a little taller than the single-story house. The tree looked half dead; there was probably more moss growing on it than leaves.

As soon as the truck stopped, Em and Marcus jumped out to take in everything. The grass made the yard look more like a field, as it stood about a foot and half high. It obviously hadn't been mowed in some time, and it was a golden color, almost the same as their Labrador, Bert, who jumped over the tailgate at about the same time they got out of the truck.

Suddenly Marcus broke the quiet as they stared in amazement at their new surroundings. "Look," he yelled, "a feather!" He was right. There was a large feather caught in a dust devil, or small, funnel-shaped gust of wind. He immediately took off after it, Bert galloping behind him and Em close on Bert's heels. The feather was huge, as far as feathers go, about eighteen inches long. It was a beautiful dark grey near the bottom, but was frosted with a silvery color that was almost translucent near the top, and it shimmered in the sunlight.

While Marcus was still admiring his new treasure, Bert started tracking some unfamiliar scent he had dis-covered. Em watched him stop, paw his new find, and then pick it up. Horrified, her eyes grew wide, and she shouted, "Snake!"

Bert gripped the snake firmly in his mouth and shook it so ferociously that everyone could hear a rattle, the telltale sound of a venomous diamondback rattlesnake. Suddenly Bert paused, and Em realized something was off. The snake was not alive; it was dried up, stiff as a board, and missing a head.

She, as well as the rest of the family, breathed a sigh of relief. Nonetheless, it was a rattlesnake, and all at once Em realized this was a very different place than she'd ever lived. She was going to need a crash course on some of the dangers in her new environment: rattlesnakes, scorpions, and tarantulas. Oh my!

After all the hubbub had quieted down, and the movers had come and gone, Dad mowed the grass. While Mom was making up all the beds, Em and Marcus unpacked their belongings. They would be sharing a room for a while. Although Em complained initially that a fourth grader shouldn't have to share a room with a first grader, Mom assured them it was only temporary. The other bedroom was filled with boxes, which needed to be unpacked, but there was just not enough time right then. Once everything was in its proper place, Marcus would have his own room. In the meantime, Em would have a first-grade roommate.

Mom inventoried the groceries and decided that she needed to investigate the mercantile. She didn't need to ask twice if anyone else wanted to accompany her; Em and Marcus both appeared out of nowhere, ready to go. Marcus was wearing an old Astros cap with his new feather proudly stuck in the side. It was quite a sight, and

Mrs. Ruiz was surprised Em wasn't complaining about being seen with him in public. Apparently, her excitement outweighed any potential embarrassment her brother might cause.

Dad had just finished mowing the lawn and warned the children one more time about the need for caution in their new habitat. The long grass clippings made an excellent hiding place for all kinds of critters. Critters or not, he was ready for a shower and then supper.

Mom said they would eat upon her return.

Chapter 3

# Introductions

The mercantile was apparently a hub of excitement in Justice. Weary travelers stopped to refuel their vehicles and stretch their legs. Evidently there wasn't another stop anywhere in the surrounding thirty to forty miles, and it looked like the mercantile had something for everyone. The snack food aisle was front and center. It was the most popular display, and it was very well stocked. It was filled with at least a dozen different kinds of jerky and dried meats, lots of chips, cookies, dill pickles, nuts, candies, and gums. It ran the whole length of the store. There was a small pizzeria in the back corner, with fountain drinks along the adjoining wall. Just about any beverage imaginable, plus a small frozen food and dairy section, was kept in a huge walk-in cooler. Additionally, a small selection of grocery items was housed in the center of the store, followed by hardware items and camping/hunting equipment in the back aisles.

Someone had ordered a pizza to go, so they evidently lived nearby. A few rough-looking ranch hands were searching for the hardware aisle, probably desperately hoping to find a necessary part without having to drive any farther. No telling how far they had come already. Everyone else seemed to be just passing through, purchasing the necessary gas, as well as the sugar and caffeine products needed to stay awake. There were several children in the snack aisle, eyeing all the goodies. Em and Marcus made room for themselves there, as well.

Mrs. Ruiz looked everything over and then grabbed a bag of nacho-cheese-flavored tortilla chips, some frozen push-ups, and another bottle of liquid soap. When she went to retrieve the children, she was somehow persuaded to purchase an additional two sticks of beef jerky, one original and one teriyaki flavored. It seemed as if everyone was ready to check out at the same time, so there was quite a gathering in front of the store's only cash register.

There was a young cowboy-looking fellow in line behind Mrs. Ruiz, and he kept looking at Marcus's cap. Em, who didn't miss much, confronted him, "Are you an Astros fan, Mister?"

The man blushed a little, knowing he had been caught, and replied, "Well, little lady, as a matter of fact, I am, but that's not what I was looking at. I was admiring that feather stuck in it."

Em's conversation immediately caught her mother's attention, and she turned around.

The stranger quickly stuck out his hand. "Pardon me, ma'am. My name is Clayton Cobb. I'm a ranger at the Choke Canyon State Park and a part-time game warden for the county. Mainly I'm just keeping an eye on the wildlife and all."

Mrs. Ruiz shook his hand. "Claire Ruiz," she replied, "and these are my children, Emeralda and Marcus."

Em stuck her hand out first. "You can call me Em," she corrected. Marcus was more bashful and didn't say a word.

Mr. Cobb shook Em's hand and then looked at Marcus. "Well, Marcus, I can tell you that feather is special. There're not too many birds around here it could belong to."

Marcus just looked at the ground. Mrs. Ruiz nudged him. "Marcus, don't be rude."

"Thank you," Marcus replied, continuing to stare at his feet.

"Well, I'll tell you what," Mr. Cobb said. "I know you'll never part with that feather now, but if you happen to find another one, let me know. I'd like to try and buy it from you. Deal?"

Marcus's head slowly started to rise, and a sly grin began to form at the corners of his mouth. "Deal," he finally answered with a full-on smile.

Just then the clerk asked, "Will this be all for you, ma'am?"

"Yes," Claire replied, and then she turned to Mr. Cobb and added, "It was nice to meet you, Mr. Cobb."

"Likewise, ma'am. And, kids, don't forget about me when you find any more of those feathers," he said as he pulled the brim of Marcus's cap down over his eyes.

Mrs. Ruiz turned back to pay the lady at the register; another man wearing a big white apron with brown smudges approached her from behind the counter.

"You're Coach Ruiz's family, aren't you? Did you just get into town?"

"Yes," Mrs. Ruiz replied surprisedly.

"Dale Dawkins," he introduced himself. "Don't be alarmed. You'll find news in a small town travels fast. We don't have too many newcomers anymore. This is my store, and I just want to welcome y'all to Justice. I got an extra pizza here, and I imagine y'all are tired, so how about it?" he asked. He handed her the pizza box.

"Thank you," she replied. "That's very kind of you."

Em's and Marcus's eyes lit up. That certainly beat cold sandwiches and nacho-cheese tortilla chips!

"Kids, I hope you like pepperoni!" he added.

"Yes, sir," Em replied, and Marcus added, "Thank you!" without even being prodded.

"It is nice to meet you, Mr. Dawkins, and thank you very much. We will certainly enjoy it," Mrs. Ruiz said as she gathered her other bag and headed out the door.

The kids were so excited that their five-minute drive home seemed like an eternity. As soon as they burst through the door, they couldn't wait to tell their father about the two men they had met and the news of the free pizza. They vividly described the men and the mercantile as they dug into the hot, cheesy pizza.

Their first day in Justice had finally ended. They had driven over a hundred miles to a totally foreign environment, found an odd-looking feather, discovered their first rattlesnake, and enjoyed a fresh, hot, delicious pizza. Now as the full moon rose over the soon-to-be track, they felt totally exhausted.

Soon the howling of coyotes filled the air—not a lone cry, but what sounded like a whole litter. They, too, seemed to be celebrating the Ruiz's arrival in Justice.

Chapter 4
# Mr. Cobb

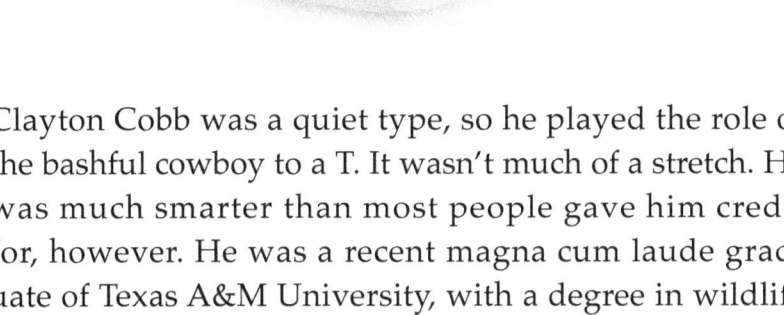

Clayton Cobb was a quiet type, so he played the role of the bashful cowboy to a T. It wasn't much of a stretch. He was much smarter than most people gave him credit for, however. He was a recent magna cum laude graduate of Texas A&M University, with a degree in wildlife management, and he was currently considering graduate work in natural resource management. His role at Choke Canyon allowed him ample time to pursue his studies, and he enjoyed it.

The canyon provided safe harbor for several species of wildlife, such as deer, javelina, alligators, wild hogs, turkeys, raccoons, opossums, skunks, coyotes, and roadrunners. It served as a resting spot for large numbers of migratory birds heading south for the winter and north for the summer. It was those migrations that had brought him to the area. He was outlining the migratory routes of whooping and sandhill cranes in Texas. A growing number of cranes wintered at the Aransas Wildlife Preserve on the

Gulf Coast and flew directly over the canyon each way. While spending time in Choke Canyon, he'd also photographed many birds of prey, some of which he could not identify. Since then, he had been trying to prove the existence of a new species of eagle.

Since the population of Kanter County was so sparse and static, it really was possible for a new species to exist there without anyone actually knowing it. After all, it would not be new to the people who lived in the area, as they would have known of it and seen it all their lives. However, it may be new to the scientific community because it had never been fully described, documented, or cataloged, and its existence had remained isolated.

Mr. Cobb would have his work cut out for him though. Not only did he need accurate photographs, but he would also have to be able to document similarities and differences with other species, including physical attributes, adaptations, diet, reproduction, and habitat. As if that weren't enough, the physical evidence he had already gathered had created even more questions than answers. Some of the feathers he had collected were too large for his species, yet he could not account for them with other species in the park either. The same thing was happening with bones he had collected to rebuild the skeletons. There appeared to be two different sizes of wings. Maybe the birds were of different ages? That still didn't explain some slight skeletal differences he'd found.

Could there be another species? If so, he had not been able to photograph it. Perhaps there had been some unusually large eagles in the area at one time. To make matters worse, all his DNA results had come back inconclusive, and there was no shortage of legends in this area. No matter what hard evidence he found, someone here had an explanation for it! According to the local community, Choke Canyon was home to prehistoric white-tailed deer, forty-foot alligators, hairless coyotes, and chupacabra. It's a wonder that *National Geographic* or *Ripley's Believe It or Not* had not done a show on this area!

Nonetheless, the stranger and more mysterious his finds, the greater his attraction for them. Perhaps he was a mystery himself. The bashful cowboy seemed to be a front for the studious scientist to hide behind.

## Chapter 5
# Bike Riding

After the children met Mr. Cobb, finding large feathers became a priority. Dollar signs began to dance in their heads. Not only did they check the yard and track every day, but they also began taking some exploration trips, much to the dismay of their mother. Although, she didn't necessarily mind the trips as much as their timing. They usually occurred while she was at work and their dad was at the gym. She had asked Em and Marcus to wait until she got home, but it was no use. Either she would be too tired to accompany them, or they would do something else.

At any rate, the children kept exploring and just didn't talk much about it. So far, they had been across the track and discovered a swampy tank. They had ridden their bikes on most of the gravel roads leading to the mercantile. With each new adventure came more confidence.

Although they had yet to find another large feather, they had come across other interesting finds. Em caught a tarantula and named it Alfredo, Freddy for short. Marcus found some more feathers for his collection. Mr. Cobb identified them as roadrunner and harrier eagle. They also found a snakeskin about two feet long. Naturally every adult to whom they showed it felt the need to remind them that somewhere there was a snake bigger than its previous skin and that they had better be careful. Other than that, they found a few pieces of flint—but no real arrowheads—and a couple of scorpions, which they avoided.

Em was ready for something new. One morning after their father left for work, she told Marcus to get ready. She went outside to catch some grasshoppers for Freddy, came back in to fill two bottles of water, and then she grabbed some empty ziplock baggies and stuffed them in her pockets just in case there was a need.

Marcus came out of their room with tennis shoes in hand and Astros cap already on.

"Hurry up and get your shoes on," Em demanded.

"What's your hurry? We've got all day," Marcus replied.

"I want to get up the hill before it gets too hot."

It was usually 100 degrees Fahrenheit before noon in Justice, and there wasn't much shade, so it was worth getting a head start in the morning.

"What's up the hill?" Marcus asked.

"A cemetery."

"A cemetery? Why do we want to go to a cemetery?"

"Oh, come on; don't be a baby!"

"I'm not a baby." Marcus stopped and frowned, disappointed that his sister would make such an accusation.

"Come on. I didn't mean anything by it," she recanted. "Mom said there was probably some old cowboy gunfighters buried there."

By the time they made it all the way up the sloping hill, it was very hot, but what they found was interesting. Although there were some normal graves, you could tell they were very old because the engraved writing was so worn. Then there were the really cool ones, too, with writing that said something like "John Doe killed in gunfight November 11, 1888" or "Horse thief hung in accordance with the law." There were also graves marked with the remnants of wooden crosses and no names. Sometimes the crosses were pretty worn, and sometimes they were simply what was left of two sticks bound with barbed wire. Even pieces of boots were staked to some of the graves. Whole boots would have probably been stolen, for sure.

The children were fascinated. Even though they did not have a lot of experience with cemeteries, they knew this place was not the norm. They knew most were lined with big cement headstones and fake flowers. There were not very many headstones here and no flowers. In fact, it was hard to tell where the lines were. The newer graves seemed to be arranged in lines, but the older ones were more haphazard.

After the children looked around for the oldest grave and came up with some pretty good ghost stories, they had had enough. By then, it was too hot, and their water was running low. Good thing the path home was downhill.

The gravel cracked and crunched under the bicycle tires, especially as the bikes picked up speed. The hot wind against their faces felt good as it dried their sweat and beat against their shirts. As they picked up even more speed, it seemed too easy to simply coast all the way home, so Em decided a little daring was needed.

She called to Marcus, "Can you ride with one hand?"

She immediately raised one of her hands, and Marcus mirrored it. That was followed by the other hand, no feet on the pedals, two handclaps, three handclaps, eyes closed, and various combinations; all the while, their tires crunched along in the gravel. They continued to pick up speed as they raced down the hill, and their laughter and frivolity increased as well. They were having so much fun; it was almost a perfect way to have spent the morning.

Then suddenly, as Em lifted her hands for yet another trick, the front bike tire caught the side of an irregular-shaped piece of rock and jerked perpendicular to the bike. Em could feel her body being propelled into the air, and she instinctively let go of her handlebars. It must have looked spectacular because all she could see was Marcus racing to keep up with her as she flew through the air. He finally came to a full stop alongside her when she hit the ground.

Em had landed on her back after almost a complete somersault, with only the hard, hot gravel to break her fall. She was stunned. It was as if all her breath had been sucked out of her lungs. She heard Marcus asking if she was okay, but she could not answer.

Marcus was getting worried and began to look around to see exactly where they had stopped.

Just as quickly as the bike tire had caught the rock, a four-wheeler sped up to the fence line along the road and skidded to a stop. Its rider was a skinny boy about Em's age; he had big, red cheeks. Little did Em and Marcus know, but what the rider lacked in size, he made up for in meanness. He was laughing at Em and yelled, "Guess they don't have gravel roads in the big city! Maybe you should have stayed at home…or put on your training wheels!"

Marcus jumped off his bike to go to his sister's defense. The four-wheeler boy turned and drove off, ambivalent to Marcus's face-off for a demanded apology. Although Marcus was only in first grade, he was a formidable fellow. He and Em were about the same size, but Marcus had been to enough football practices during his short life that he was already an adept tackler, and he never backed down.

Now Marcus didn't know what to do. He was furious. Not only did this kid laugh at his sister, but he also didn't even offer to help, and she might really be hurt. Fortunately for him, he wasn't the only one who was mad.

Em had heard everything. Although she hadn't been able to respond, tears welled up in her eyes, more from the insult than the pain. Bruises, cuts, and scratches would heal, but her pride had taken an even-more-severe blow, and to Em, that was much worse.

When Marcus saw the tears, he really got worried. Em NEVER cried. "Em," he asked, "are you all right?"

"Yes," she gasped, still not moving.

"Are you sure?"

Then she steadied herself on a bloodied elbow, and Marcus carefully helped her to her feet. He tried to dust her off, but she wouldn't allow it—not there!

"Let's go home," she said.

"But your elbow is bleeding…and your knee too."

"We can take care of it at home," she insisted. "Let's go. I'll make it fine." She shot an evil glance in the direction the four-wheeler had gone and then turned to join her brother.

Chapter 6

# A Rattler

Em did not forget the mean boy she and Marcus had encountered on their way home from the cemetery. His sunburned cheeks and harsh laugh had made a lasting impression. She had no desire to see him again, yet she knew she would. This was, after all, a small town. She was not quite sure how she would handle their next face-off, but it wouldn't be pretty. An accidental trip in a school hallway was way too nice—unless maybe it was into broken glass or dog poop. One thing was for sure; this kid had no idea what kind of mortal enemy he had made.

Em decided that she and Marcus had done enough exploring for a while, so she convinced him to play on the track for a while that morning. She promised him that once it got hot, they could go inside and play video games. Thank goodness Dad had finally found the time to get the video equipment unpacked and set up, even if temporarily, in their room. She couldn't imagine how kids here lived without video games.

They took out their bubble guns and kites, and of course their water bottles. They ran for a while, playing Olympic races, sealing their victories by pouring their water over their heads. Then they chased each other with heavy bubble fire. Bert came out to chase the bubbles with them, and when they all got tired, the kites were released into the breezes. The wind was always blowing in Justice, as it wasn't that far from the Gulf Coast. It was just that sometimes the wind wasn't any cooler than the sun itself.

Bert had lumbered off somewhere, probably to find some shade. The heat had been particularly hard on him and his old age, and the children had temporarily forgotten about him. That is, until he started barking. Bert hardly ever barked, so he really caught their attention.

"Where is he?" asked Marcus.

"Over there," Em answered as she pointed to the tank just beyond the track. "Look at those buzzards circling over him. What do you think he's got?"

"I don't know, but whatever it is, it must be dead," Marcus replied.

"Not yet. The buzzards are still circling, waiting. Let's go!" Em took off.

Marcus grabbed their water bottles and pursued her. As they ran toward the tank, they could see Bert barking toward another fence line, or at least where the fence was supposed to be. Something had torn down the barbed wire and was entangled in the mess.

Em called Bert off, but he wouldn't budge, so Marcus grabbed him by the collar and pulled him back.

"It's a baby horse!" Em yelled.

The horse lay very still. It may have been young, but it already appeared to be bigger than the children. It was badly tangled in the barbed wire and looked severely dehydrated.

"Is it dead?" Marcus asked.

"I'm not sure," Em answered. "It has fire ants on it too." Those meddlesome ants seemed to live everywhere and stung like crazy. "We must get them off first. I don't know how long this guy has been here, but we've got to help him."

Marcus kept his distance, unsure of touching a dead animal.

As Em gently brushed off the ants, the horse let out a soft whinny. "It's alive," she announced half amazed.

With life confirmed, Marcus hurried to help his sister.

"Careful," she warned. "Don't let the ants get on you."

"Imagine how this poor little guy feels," Marcus empathized. His protective instinct kicked in again. It made no difference whether man or beast was in peril.

"Do you still have some water?" Em asked.

"It's over by Bert."

"Go get it. Maybe it will help. I'm sure he's thirsty." As Em began carefully unwrapping the barbed wire, she found another big feather tangled in the mess, and then another.

As Marcus walked over to Bert to retrieve the water bottle, he realized something else was wrong. Bert was intent on something new, but this time he was not barking. In fact, he was deadly still. He appeared stiff and rigid, like a statue. Marcus paused cautiously.

"Bert," he called, "c'mere, boy!"

There was still no movement, not even a hint of recognition. Now Marcus knew something was wrong. Then he heard it. What was it? It was a familiar sound. He had heard it before. It was the sound he had heard when they first arrived at their new home, when Bert shook that dead snake in his mouth... It was a rattle!

"Em?" Marcus called with just a bit of panic in his voice.

Em hadn't detected the tone, as she was preoccupied with the hurt foal. "Hurry up," she said impatiently. "Throw the bottle to me."

Marcus scanned the area. He couldn't see a snake, but he knew it would be camouflaged in these surroundings. The water bottle was behind Bert. Marcus carefully and slowly grabbed it and threw it toward his sister.

Em still was oblivious to Marcus's new drama. She picked up the water bottle and poured some water in her hand, carefully holding it to the horse's lips.

It licked it out of her hand and opened its eyes. It began to rustle, but it was still restrained by some wire.

Em quickly continued to unwrap the animal, but as she turned him over, there was another surprise. A wing. She stopped. Did one of the buzzards get caught in here too? That would be gross. It was hard to tell with all the feathers underneath the horse. They looked too light-colored to be a buzzard's feathers. She summoned up her bravery and started to remove the wire again to get a closer look, but suddenly Marcus got her attention. She knew he was blubbering about something, and then she heard him say, "Snake."

"Em," Marcus repeated, "it's a rattlesnake!"

As soon as Em heard the word, she was on her feet. "Marcus, get away!"

"I've got to get Bert. He won't budge."

"Leave him. He'll be okay. He's a dog. He'll know what to do."

"No, he hasn't seen these snakes before." He reached out to grab Bert's collar, as he had done before, but Bert turned to him and growled. Bert had never growled at either of the children, but he was only trying to get Marcus away from the danger.

Unfortunately, the sudden movement of Bert's head triggered the snake to strike, and it sank its fangs into the side of Bert's jowls. Marcus watched helplessly. Horrified, he grabbed Bert's collar just as Em reached him. The snake had recoiled for strike two.

"Be still," Em commanded.

Bert's face began to swell. Tears were streaming down Marcus's cheeks. He was not like Em. He totally bared his emotions. "Bert's been bit, Em. What do we do now?"

"I'm not sure; just be still."

## Chapter 7
# The Secret

For once in her life, Em honestly did not know what to do. The immediate danger was in front of her, but she felt something behind her as well. She could not look though. She did not want to make any unnecessary movement whatsoever. A shadow crept over her. What was going on?

The small horse had untangled itself from the wire Em had loosened. Maybe it wasn't a baby after all. It nuzzled her to the side and then suddenly reared on its two hind hooves, spreading its huge gossamer wings. One stretched in front of Bert, and the snake immediately struck at it. Its wings were twice as long as Em's arms and much more powerful. They beat the air, shimmering dust falling from them.

Em stood amazed. It was as if they were suddenly inside a magical rainbow. This couldn't be happening.

With its awesome display, the horse took on the snake's full-frontal attack.

Marcus seized the moment and grabbed Bert. "C'mon, Em. We've got to go now, while the snake is distracted." Marcus wiped the dust off his face and pulled at Bert.

The dog let out a whimper. He did not seem to mind the dust as much as the bite.

Em did not move. She was dumbfounded.

"C'mon, Em; help me!" Marcus was struggling with Bert while the tears kept falling from his eyes and trickling down his cheeks. "Em!" he screamed.

She began to follow, but still had not fully snapped out of it. Did Marcus not witness the same thing she had? "Marcus," she said, "that was not a baby horse."

"I don't care. I don't care what it was. Bert is bit badly, and you know rattlesnakes are deadly. I don't want him to die, Em. I don't want Bert to die," he pleaded again. "Please help me get him to Mom. She'll know what to do." He turned and headed back home.

"Mom's at work," Em stated matter-of-factly, as her mind was still trying to process the amazing scene they had just witnessed. "What about the horse-thingy?"

She didn't wait for an answer. She knew he was right. Bert was more important than an animal they had just found, no matter how spectacular.

"I don't care if she's at work. She has a phone. I'll call her! What don't you get? We have to hurry! We should probably try to carry him."

Logic was returning to Em. "Marcus, we cannot carry Bert. He is way too big, and you're right; it is probably not a good idea for him to run. It will pump the poison through his body that much faster. He's a dog, though, a big one at that." She reassured Marcus, "Dogs can handle snakebites better than people." Or at least she thought so. "Let's just keep him comfortable and walk him back to the house. There is no immediate danger." She turned to look back. The horse was gone. She was not sure about the snake, but they were far enough away from it for it not to be a concern.

They reached the edge of the track and kept going. Em's mind was in overdrive from all the excitement. "Marcus, do you know what a Pegasus is?"

"A what-a-sus?"

"You know, like the horse Hercules rode in the Disney movie?"

"Oh yeah, but I don't know if that was what we found."

"But it did have wings, right? Whatever it was, it definitely had wings."

"Yeah, it had wings, but I don't know what it was," he said unaffectedly. "Should we take Bert inside?"

"Don't you think Mom will freak?" Em answered, still trying to make sense of what just happened.

"I'll call her."

"What are you going to tell her?"

"Duh. That Bert got bit by a rattlesnake!" he said incredulously.

"Oh yeah, that won't make her freak," she said sarcastically.

They finally reached their yard. Em stopped to look at Bert closely. "I thought his face was swelling. Look, it doesn't look so bad anymore." She brushed off some of the glittery dust that was still on Bert's face, and he did not whimper this time.

"What if all the poison has spread from his face to the rest of his body?" Marcus asked.

"Well, I don't think he would still be standing here with us then, right?"

Marcus thought about it. If the poison had spread throughout Bert's body, he would be a lot worse off. Em was right. He did look somewhat better. "You can still see the fang marks and a little dried blood."

"Well, they'll have to scab over just like any other bite or cut."

"I still think we need to call Mom," he concluded.

Chapter 8

# Myth or Reality

The next day was Sunday, and everything had returned to normal. Bert was lying on the mat in front of the back door when they woke up, and he was ready for his breakfast as usual. Not the typical behavior of a dog on his deathbed from a rattlesnake bite.

Mom assured them that Bert was fine. She could see the fang marks, so she knew the children were telling the truth about the snakebite, but she wasn't convinced it had been a rattlesnake.

"Mom," Em pleaded their case, "it is possible for an adult rattlesnake to control the amount of venom it injects. Maybe the snake decided not to inject venom into Bert."

"Em, the snake was using a defense mechanism. Why would it not inject venom? A snake is a snake. It is incapable of logical thought. It does not stop and think, 'Oh, what a nice dog; maybe I won't inject my venom into him.' Look, regardless of what kind of snake it was, I am sure you were both scared witless, as well you should be, wandering off out there by yourselves."

Em could feel the lecture coming on again and changed the topic away from the snake. "I know, Mom, we are really sorry, but what about the Pegasus we might have found?"

This subject was not any better though. "Em, you know a Pegasus is a MYTHICAL creature. It does not exist in Justice, or anywhere else, for that matter. It was just a made-up story." Em had worn her down a bit. She had conceded that it was possible, although highly unlikely, that a rattlesnake could bite without injecting venom, but she drew the line at believing in mythical creatures. "A Pegasus…really? You must be mistaken. Imagine all that adrenaline pumping through your body from all the excitement and fear. Who wouldn't be—"

"Scared enough to see a mythical creature?" Em completed her question. "I wouldn't be."

"Just get ready for church, please. You can take me out to where all of this happened this afternoon, okay?"

"Okay."

Em had a better plan, though. As soon as church was over, she cornered Mr. Cobb. She knew he would know more about the wildlife in this area than anyone else. However, she had to first decide whether he could be trusted and with how much information. She knew she already had her hands full trying to convince her parents; she did not want to bring any more nonbelievers into this.

"Hello, Mr. Cobb. Do you remember me from the mercantile?" she asked.

"Why, if it isn't Miss Emeralda Ruiz— Oh, I'm sorry. It was Em, right?" He winked.

"Yes, sir." She smiled, glad he remembered her.

"I was wondering if I could ask you some questions?"

"Of course, little lady, what's on your mind?"

"Well," she said, suddenly turning more serious, "I was wondering if you believed in *la chupacabra*? I've heard a lot about them." She felt bad about lying, it being at church and all, but it was for the greater good, she reasoned.

"Why?" he asked. "Are you afraid?"

"No, no. It's nothing like that," she assured him. "It's just that I was wondering if you believe that they exist because, you know, no one can prove they exist. It is just a legend, right?" She obviously knew nothing of Mr. Cobb's research.

"We-ell," he said with a rather long drawl and a smile, "I guess that's true, but no one has ever proven that they don't exist either. Now, I don't want to scare you, so let's change the subject to pink and purple polka-dotted deer." He winked again.

Em wasn't sure where he was going with that, but so far she had a winner.

"Let's say, for instance, I can prove that pink and purple polka-dotted deer don't exist. No one has ever seen one.

No one has ever heard of one. No one has ever found evidence of one, right?"

"Right," she played along.

"Okay, now for the chupacabra's case... Again, don't be scared. This is all for the sake of argument, but there have been reports, questionable photos, and anecdotes. No hard evidence, though. You know, stuff that would stand up in the scientific community's judgment, so the jury is still out. Maybe we just haven't looked in the right place for evidence? Only time will tell."

"What if I found evidence of something no one else has ever seen?" she asked.

"How would you know if you didn't see it?"

"I saw it," she answered.

"You think you saw a chupacabra?"

"No, but you know those feathers you like—"

"Em"—her mother waved from across the rapidly-diminishing crowd—"we need to leave. Your dad needs to get on the road to San Antonio for the basketball shoot-out this afternoon." She saw Mr. Cobb and walked over. "Hello, Mr. Cobb. Has Em been giving you an earful?"

"No, ma'am. We're just talking." Mr. Cobb smiled genuinely.

"M-om!" Em cautioned as her eyes grew about three sizes, and she shot her mother a glance that said, "Stop embarrassing me."

"No doubt about her Pegasus sighting," her mother continued. "Em does have an active imagination, but in her defense, I'm sure the children were scared witless. Anyhow, you can tell him all about it later. Your dad needs to get going. We'll see you later, Mr. Cobb." She turned Em around by the shoulders and led her across the church-yard to the truck.

Em turned around and waved goodbye to Mr. Cobb. "I'll explain later," she mouthed.

Clayton Cobb pushed his hat back on his head and rubbed his forehead. What just happened? His mind was racing as he replayed the conversation in his head. What was Em trying to tell him? Had she seen a Pegasus? What about the feathers; did they belong to a winged horse? They were mythical creatures, right? Greek or Roman? Not Texan, no. Maybe… He wasn't so sure anymore. After all, he had several large skeletal bones he couldn't place—hollow, suggesting flight, too large for his eagle. No way... Suddenly he wanted to go home.

"Mr. Cobb," Brother Jeff called, "will we see you at Tio's for lunch?"

"I'm afraid not, Brother Jeff. My stomach is a little queasy. I think I'll just head home."

"Well, we'll miss you. Hope you feel better."

"Yes, sir. I'm sure I will."

Chapter 9

# Someone to Trust

As soon as he got home, Clayton searched the Internet for every possible Pegasus fact or legend he could find, and he still couldn't decide if it was a purely mythical creature or not. Is that what Emeralda Ruiz was trying to ask? Several carnival showmen had claimed to have a Pegasus skeleton on display, but they always ended up being hoaxes.

On a sidenote, he had seen that the name *Pegasus* came from a word that meant spring or fountain, and stories said that everywhere the winged horse's hoof struck earth, a spring burst forth. Legend? Of course. It had to be. Was it a coincidence, then, that prior to being settled in the mid-nineteenth century, small, beaver-filled springs dotted the countryside of Kanter County? Those springs helped the streams of the canyon flow all year round. Could their existence have been linked to an animal? Could a mythical creature impact the real environment? That didn't make any sense.

He rummaged through his previous research and turned his study upside down. He rechecked historical records, old census reports, county archives, and old newspaper articles. He could find no mention of winged horses, but, then, the natives of South Texas would probably not call such creatures Pegasi. That, after all, was a Greek reference. What would such creatures be called in South Texas? He didn't know.

He ran across several lists of indigenous animals that were no longer seen. It included panthers, beavers, and wild horses. Although he knew panthers were rare, one could be seen every few years or so. They were often mistaken for bobcats, which were plentiful. However, he had never seen any beavers or wild horses. Could their fates be linked? After all, many of the springs and small streams had dried up. Were the wild horses merely horses, or something more perhaps? So many of these questions he could not answer, and early written historical records were sparse. Thieves and outlaws weren't known for their historical or scientific accounts. But perhaps, still, the most pressing question was what did Emeralda Ruiz see?

Several days passed, and he was still not any closer to getting any of the answers for which he was searching. The problem now became how to find out what Em knew. If he tried to be sly and get the information surreptitiously, someone in the community might get the wrong idea. This was still a small town with small-town gossip, so that would be a bad idea.

Clayton figured honesty was the best policy. Unfortunately, it was difficult to tell someone you might believe her story that Pegasi exist, without appearing to be a nut-case yourself. Is that what he believed? He wasn't sure.

Clayton decided to approach it from the totally logical perspective of investigating claims of a new species of animal without a name. After all, that's exactly what he was doing. He had pictures of bones and droppings, which were documented and dated. He was just trying to find out what Em had seen and if it might be useful in his investigation. With that thought, he gathered up his courage and knocked on the front door of the Ruiz home.

Mrs. Ruiz answered and invited him in. He had called earlier and asked if he could come over and talk to Em about what she had seen. He explained that he had another account of a wild horse, and he wanted to compare details to see if this was a new animal in the area or perhaps a ranch runaway, or maybe even a runaway that had gone feral. He thought that sounded perfectly logical.

"Well, if you ask me," Coach Ruiz interjected, "I think the children just got a little carried away. Their imaginations have gone on all kinds of adventures since we moved here. From the Olympics to safaris, they've imagined it all. They were probably just playing, and that snake scared them so badly that they confused their reality."

"I know what I saw, Dad," Em replied while rolling her eyes. "I'm not a little kid anymore," she protested.

"What snake?" Mr. Cobb asked.

The children explained how the rattler had struck Bert, but by the time they got home, the swelling had all but disappeared. "I think it might have something to do with the dust. It shook from the animal's wings like salt from a shaker, except it was very, very fine, almost mist-like."

"What are you talking about, Em?" her mother asked. "You never mentioned any of this."

"Because you didn't believe me. The wings of a Pegasus are very powerful. I've read that they could be used as vicious weapons, as well as nurturing appendages. Some people even believe that their wings had magical powers. I think they might have healed Bert."

"Look, Em, I know you are a very smart girl with a wonderful imagination, but if Mr. Cobb here is serious about researching the possibility of some new animal, he can't exactly make scientific claims about an animal with magical powers. Science and magic don't exactly mix. You need to be honest with him."

"I am, Mom. I know it sounds crazy, but I just want to tell the whole story."

"And I appreciate that, Ms. Em," Clayton said, and he nodded at Mrs. Ruiz to signal it was okay.

"Mr. Cobb," Marcus said, finally gathering the courage to speak, "I think it was more like teeny-tiny feathers because they kind of floated when they fell from his wings."

"Okay, son. You and your sister go in the other room now and let the grown-ups talk," Dad said.

"Mr. Cobb, I appreciate your interest, and—who knows?—maybe the kids did stumble across a wild horse or something. But you're not buying all of this, are you? I mean, you're not putting any real weight on their story, right? I just don't want you to get your hopes up. Remember, they are just kids, and my kids tend to be imaginative."

Mrs. Ruiz added, "Their story is pretty wild, even for us to hear, and, believe me, we have heard some doozies!"

"I appreciate your concern, and, believe me, I am concerned also. I certainly do not want to ruin my reputation as a wildlife scientist by making wild assertions, so I'm not ready to jump on board yet, but I would like to investigate further. I already have pieces that don't belong to any normal puzzle." He showed them his pictures.

"Now, I'm not saying they found a magical horse, but there is too much here to ignore. Would you mind if the kids took me to the place of all this excitement, so I could look around? Maybe there is something there that could help explain all this logically once and for all. Believe me, I am a creature of logic. Any evidence, at this point, would be helpful to either confirm or refute their story. I would like to see if I could perhaps find that snake, dead or alive. That alone might answer some questions about their story, like if it was really a rattler? Would you mind if I took them out tomorrow morning?" Mr. Cobb asked.

"Well, I'll be at work, so it's up to you guys. Just, please, keep an eye on them," said Mrs. Ruiz.

"I don't mind at all," added Coach, "but what if you do find something?"

"Simple—photograph, document, and protect. I certainly don't want to interfere with something that has managed to be anonymous this long."

"Just making sure my kids don't bring home a new pet!" Coach Ruiz laughed.

His wife's eyes widened. "Oh, I didn't think of that. Definitely no new pets."

"No problem," Mr. Cobb replied with a smile.

Chapter 10

# The Search Begins

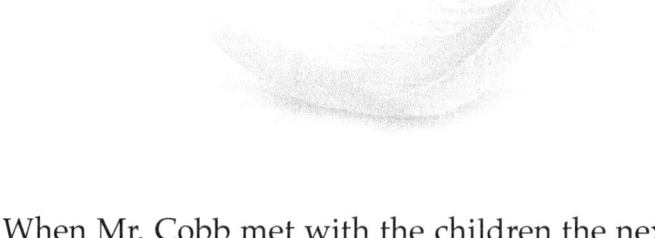

When Mr. Cobb met with the children the next morning, their mission was simple: to listen to their story completely, without interruption, and retrace their exact, or close to exact, steps as best they could remember. Em gave a thorough account, and Marcus chimed in when he felt Em had neglected significant details. The children led Mr. Cobb to the exact spot where all the excitement had occurred.

First, Mr. Cobb examined the barbed wire. He was more than a little excited at what he found, but he kept his wits about him, especially since he was in front of the children. He took at least a dozen photographs of the tangled wire from different angles. Then he slipped on some gloves and examined pieces of it in greater detail. Some of the barbs had retained bits of the animal's hide and knots of hair. Upon closer examination, he found a smudge of blood, perhaps from the animal's struggle against the wire restraint.

Each piece of evidence was labeled, placed in a plastic bag, documented in his notebook, and then carefully placed in his backpack. He found the kids' water bottle and asked if he could borrow it for a while. Then they tracked down the nearest fire-ant mound, and Mr. Cobb documented, photographed, and marked its location on a rough map he had drawn of the area. Additionally, he took several soil samples from each site. Finally, he turned his attention to the snake hunt.

Mr. Cobb was no stranger to snakes, and he was prepared. He took from his backpack two metal tubes about the size of paper-towel rolls and handed them to the kids. "These are telescopic walking sticks," he explained. He showed them how to pull them out to their full length of five feet, a little taller than Em. "Some of the bigger snakes can strike five feet, but hopefully we would see one that size well in advance. I don't want you touching anything. Poke it first. Keep your stick in front of you. If you accidentally surprise a snake, he'll be upset. Use the stick, always keep your distance, and call for help. Do we understand each other?"

He had given them careful instructions. All their senses should be on alert. Ears listening for any possible sound, from a rattle to a rustle. Eyes on the ground, poised to notice any movement or difference in camouflage. Noses ready to pick up any scent. They would not smell a snake, but they might smell a dead animal, snake or otherwise. And touch…if they happened to step on something strange, look out! Everything should be poked first! With noon approaching, if there was a snake around, it would be searching for a shady crevice or rocky ledge to hide under.

Before they even got started, Em found a pile of droppings and was curious. "Mr. Cobb, what kind of droppings are these? They look like almond M&M's without the candy coating."

"Or dull Sugar Babies," Marcus added.

They all laughed.

Mr. Cobb answered, "I wouldn't eat those—that's deer poop!" He grinned. "I guess you are right, though; they could pass for candy if someone wanted to trick you. Better be nice to your sister," he said jokingly as he winked at Marcus. "Now, let's spread out and get to work."

They had only gone about fifty yards when Marcus called, "I found something!"

It was a headless body of a snake that looked as if it had been run over by a car. It looked almost identical to the one Bert had found when they moved in. But the most important thing about the snake's lifeless body was the fact that there were eight rattles on the end of the tail. The children were right; it was a rattlesnake.

Mr. Cobb photographed the dead snake; then he carefully turned it over and photographed some more. Finally, he picked it up and placed it in yet another baggie, labeled it, and documented it in his notebook. He took another soil sample and calmly told the children he appreciated all their help, but he thought he'd found all he could for the day.

He was totally professional about the whole thing, not showing any emotion as to whether he had confirmed their story or not. Em and Marcus did not know what to think, but Mr. Cobb's backpack was full.

Unbeknownst to the children, Mr. Cobb was amazed. He kept his feelings in check, though, because he was determined to make a totally objective conclusion. He was careful to preserve all his evidence so that his results could be verified and not compromised. Some of the hide samples had skin tags that could be analyzed for DNA. Perhaps the bloody wire could be sampled as well. The specimens had to be carefully packed and sent back to the university, and only time would tell.

In the meantime, Mr. Cobb was determined to gather some additional evidence. He needed a sighting. He had to see whatever this was with his own eyes. He wasn't sure how something this size could be so elusive. His next job, then, was to figure out a way to see this creature. Obviously, whatever species this was, it was good at not being noticed. Certainly, any discovery of this magnitude would have spread like wildfire across the county, so why hadn't it been seen?

His first thought was to set up video surveillance cameras, but several obstacles had to be overcome first. The equipment he needed would be expensive. It would have to be battery or solar powered. After all, there were no outlets to plug into in the middle of the brush. It would also have to be equipped with night vision. Any flashing or artificial light source would obviously draw attention to itself and possibly deter his subject. Additionally, it would have to be camouflaged. But perhaps the biggest concern was where he would locate it.

With all that fresh in his mind, Mr. Cobb began his search. Finding the equipment would just be the beginning; installation, night watches, and hours of watching film or developing pictures would soon follow. What was he getting into?

## Chapter 11
# School

School registration wasn't at all what Em was expecting. In fact, she and Marcus appeared to be the only ones there, besides several prekindergarten-aged children.

"Only new students need to register. Returning students were preregistered in the spring, so you two are probably it, besides the pre-K kiddos, of course," Mr. Bigsby, the principal, explained to their mother. "We don't get a huge influx of new students around here."

Marcus breathed a sigh of relief. The longer he could put off social interactions, the better.

Em was a little disappointed that she couldn't meet anyone in her class. "Can we at least meet our teachers?" she asked.

"Let's see. Some of them are here today, working in their rooms. Em is in the fourth grade. That is Ms. Tejeda's class. I believe she is here. I'll walk you down."

As they walked down the hall, Em couldn't help but notice how clean everything was. It was bright and shiny, ready for the kids.

"Here we are. Knock, Knock," Mr. Bigsby announced their arrival.

A friendly, dark-haired lady was sitting in the corner among several stacks of books. She propped half-glasses on top of her head and looked up.

"I have one of your students here, Ms. Tejeda. She wanted to meet you. This is—"

"Em Ruiz, I'll bet," she finished his sentence, pulled herself to her feet, and extended her hand.

Em was surprised as she reached out to shake her hand. "How did you know?" she asked surprisedly.

"Well, you're number six, and I know the other five."

"What?" Em asked with a puzzled look on her face.

Ms. Tejeda looked amused. "We will have six students in our class this year. The other five students were in third grade last year, so I knew who they were, but I haven't had the pleasure of meeting you yet. I have, however, met your father. I am glad to finally meet you. I hope you will enjoy my class."

Em smiled politely. "I've never been in such a small class before."

Marcus had been silent the whole time, hoping to go unnoticed.

However, Ms. Tejeda couldn't allow that; she ventured a friendly hello.

He backed up a little, hoping to find shelter behind Em, but felt his mother's eyes, so he quietly said hello.

"What grade are you in?" she asked.

Marcus looked at his shoes as if the answer were written on his laces. "First," he replied.

"My daughter, Tina, is in the first grade too."

His mother entered the conversation. She reassuringly placed her hands on his shoulders and said, "We are hoping to meet Marcus's teacher next. We didn't mean to interrupt you. We just wanted to meet you and see where the class was. I appreciate your time."

Ms. Tejeda wiped her brow for dramatic effect. "Sometimes it's good to be interrupted." She smiled at the children and winked. "I'll see you on the first day of school."

"Next stop, Ms. K.," Mr. Bigsby announced.

They passed the restrooms, walked down one door, and on the opposite side of the hall was an open door. Next to it, there was a paper tree with nine apples. Marcus's name was on one of the apples. Marcus was glad his class was close to Em's.

Again Mr. Bigsby repeated his routine and poked his head in with a hello.

A quirky, little lady with wiry, grey hair popped out of the closet. She had bright-blue eyes just like Marcus's, but she was very loud. "Hello, hello, hello. Who have we here? Oh my goodness, look at these spiderwebs on me! Have you ever seen anything like that? Dirty old closet! Don't worry, though; I'm pulling out all the good stuff!" She took off her glasses and wiped them on her shirt, not pausing a moment. "Let me dust myself off and come over and give you a hug!"

Marcus was petrified. He couldn't even duck for cover. This lady didn't stop talking or hugging, and he wasn't big on either. He didn't even like shaking hands. No matter, though, because here she was, hugging him—and not only him, but Mom and Em too. He heard his mother speak, but by then everything was a blur. He had totally withdrawn from the conversation.

Thankfully, his mother understood that he was over-whelmed. He was glad when they left, but was dreading the first day of school even more.

Chapter 12

# Summer's End

For the kids, everything was pretty much over. They had presented their case, and now the jury was out. Waiting is never easy for children, and it was killing Em. She was expecting a call from Mr. Cobb every day to tell her that she had done it, that he could prove she had seen a Pegasus, but that call didn't come.

As for Marcus, he had all but forgotten the incident. Perhaps it was the shock of it all, but his attention was focused on the dwindling days of summer vacation's freedom and the encroachment of school bringing the drudgery of homework. He was not at all excited about the start of school. Unlike Em, this would be his first real year in school, and nothing about this school appealed to him. It didn't even have a football team. What would they do on Friday nights? Not to mention, he would have to sit in school for eight hours a day—no more daytime television, no more video games for hours on end, no more mornings lounging in pajamas at Grandma's house or lunches with Grandpa, no more bicycle adventures. This was going to be awful!

Em normally loved school, even a new one. She was a pro at starting over; her dad was a coach, for crying out loud. She was used to moving, but even she was not excited about the upcoming school year. The thought of being inaccessible for eight hours a day bothered her. How would Mr. Cobb contact her? What if the Pegasus returned? What was she going to do to the mean kid? No, she never forgot.

As the start of school approached, so the change of seasons approached too. Probably for most of the nation this meant the green of summer began to fade and trans-form into autumn oranges, reds, and golds, but not in South Texas—autumn did not really exist here. If there were any greens left that happened to survive the South Texas sun, they would gradually continue to fade until the first frost, probably in December. The traditional autumn colors here were just even-more-faded greens, grays, and browns, and instead of one-hundred-degree highs, temperatures usually only rose to the eighties and nine-ties. More importantly, in Justice autumn meant hunting season was approaching.

The town was getting ready for its great transforma-tion. Professional hunting guides were arriving, stocking up on supplies, and leaving cards and flyers in all the obvious and not-so-obvious places. The mercantile was bustling. There were extra displays for school supplies, as well as camouflage hats, gloves, shirts, jackets, pants, and even long underwear. Corners and endcaps were filled with ammunition, No Scent sprays, hand warmers, gas lanterns, gun scopes, batteries, and flashlights. The beer coolers were stocked to capacity. The gas station in front of the mercantile even had a line early some mornings and at dusk. Feeders and blinds for sale began to appear in parking lots and along roadsides. Even the sole restaurant in town seemed to pick up its pace. As more and more people were coming into town to get ready for school, rest, or to stock up, business was booming. It began to look more like a town—kind of a Rambo meets Bambi sort of town, but a town nonetheless.

Chapter 13

# The Waiting Game

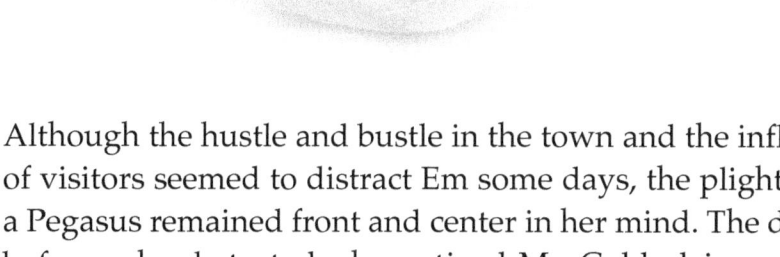

Although the hustle and bustle in the town and the influx of visitors seemed to distract Em some days, the plight of a Pegasus remained front and center in her mind. The day before school started, she noticed Mr. Cobb drive past their house and into the brush with a strange contraption in the bed of his truck. That was all the invitation she needed to tag along.

Mr. Cobb was hauling a metal hunting blind in two pieces. He had wanted to set it up midday when he thought he would not be seen; everyone would be either at work or inside due to the heat. Of course, he knew by now that nothing escaped Em's notice.

After Mr. Cobb assembled the blind in a brushy area, he and Em gathered more brush around it and up its base. Mr. Cobb had painted it with the tan, gray, and brown colors, and they covered any sharp corners with burlap. Solar panels, cameras, recorders, and various other pieces of audiovisual equipment were mounted onto the blind and hidden. They sprayed No Scent to remove any human odors and brushed away footprints with a handful of long weeds.

They worked up quite a sweat in the unforgiving heat. Mr. Cobb had some cool water in an ice chest. Em had never tasted anything so good.

Mr. Cobb was all business, though. Everything was always done in steps and photographed. Even the most mundane chores were documented. He told Em he still didn't know anything, and her disappointment was obvious.

"What if someone thinks it is a deer and shoots it?" All the guides coming into town to scout out their leases couldn't be good for their efforts.

"Well, first, hunting season won't start for a couple of months. They are just putting out feed now; maybe that will help us. Plus, no one has seen it except you. It would be good to have another sighting; it doesn't matter by whom. It would provide credibility for your story. Don't forget they can't start shooting yet."

He sounded very reassuring. Unfortunately, Mr. Cobb, too, was worried. He wasn't worried about the creature getting shot because a body would certainly be proof the animal had existed. He was more concerned about it being scared away.

Chapter 14

# Results

When the phone rang, Mr. Cobb thought nothing of it. But when he heard the voice on the other end of the line, he knew something was in the works.

"Mr. Cobb, Dr. Jack Fletcher here from the Department of Biomedical Science at Texas A&M University. I understand you have something down your way breaking through fences and getting those ranchers up in arms."

That was Mr. Cobb's story. He'd told the researchers to whom he had sent his samples that he needed to find out what kind of animal had been breaking fences so that he could set an effective trap to relocate the perpetrator. But Mr. Cobb had heard nothing, not even a confirmation of the receipt of his request, and now he had Dr. Fletcher on his phone. He should have a received a rather dry, poorly-written form letter from some poor undergraduate student explaining the backlog of work. He knew because he used to have to write them.

But now he was speaking to a Dr. Fletcher, head of something or other, not even a peon grad student. He had found something that got somebody's attention. Now he had to find out who and what before the researchers found out where.

"Yes, sir," he replied matter-of-factly. "Any idea what I'm looking for?"

"Well, no, not exactly. We were kind of hoping you could shed some more light on the mystery," the voice answered. "Has anybody seen anything?"

"No, sir," he replied. "That's why I'm not sure what to try. Thought maybe some kids might be causing all the trouble, but wanted to see what the evidence said." He was fishing now to see what he could find out.

"Hmmm," Dr. Fletcher continued, "well, have you had any more reports?"

Mr. Cobb was not sure how to handle this question. He didn't want to answer no and have the investigation stall, but he didn't want to answer yes and appear to have a huge problem on his hands either.

"Not sure—haven't heard of any more problems, but sometimes these ranchers take matters into their own hands. There are a lot of fences down here that don't get checked very often. I know I have one angry rancher on my hands; I wasn't really looking for any more, if you know what I mean." Now it was his turn to try again. "So was there something wrong with the samples I sent? No disrespect intended, but I usually don't get a phone call. Can I rule out kids?" He knew nothing was wrong with the samples; the good doctor would not be wasting his time.

"No, no. The samples were good, we think…just not what we were expecting for your part of the country. Do you have any big monitors down there?"

Surprised again. "As in lizards?" He had never even considered a big lizard.

"The blood, tissue, and saliva samples are loaded with antimicrobial peptides and anticoagulants, or blood thinners. I've never seen a mixture like this. It is as if this animal can defend itself from any number of bites or infections while delivering a bite that will cause virtually any creature to bleed to death, yet it doesn't cause itself to bleed…kind of like Komodo dragons, maybe? I'd swear the samples were contaminated, except for the simple fact that these antibodies simply don't exist in nature. Even the dragon's mixture is different. I've only seen some of the modified versions in laboratories developing vaccines. Now it looks as if we are stumbling upon another one of Mother Nature's natural brews."

He continued, "Scientists have been studying big lizards like the Komodo dragons and Gila monsters for years, trying to figure out what natural-antibody blend they possess to protect themselves from their virulent saliva. I could theorize that you are looking for a big lizard. It must be large to get caught in a barbed-wire fence! The DNA evidence from the hair was inconclusive. It looked like some sort of horse, but it could have been from a domesticated horse and just happened to have been on that part of the fence. But, then again, those Komodo dragons have been known to bring down water buffalo, so perhaps you're looking for a big lizard that brought down a horse. Again, the problem I have with that theory is that these samples were gathered in South Texas, and the Komodo dragon is thousands of miles away in Indonesia! Gila monsters are closer, but not nearly big enough. It just doesn't make any sense! If there were lizards that size in Texas, surely, we would have heard about it by now."

Mr. Cobb was stunned. "You're right; that doesn't make any sense. I've never heard of any big monitors in Texas… or in North America, for that matter. Are there any?"

"The Gila monster is in the Southwestern United States. I don't think in Texas, though. Even so, it is very small compared to the size of monitor you would be looking for. But that brings up another subject of interest to us. The Gila monster's saliva has been used to develop new drugs to treat diabetes. Imagine the possibilities of drugs that could be developed from your animal's blood, sweat, tears, saliva, etc. We could be looking at cures for cancer, autoimmune disorders, influenza, and maybe even COVID."

Then it clicked. This was a doctor of biomedical research. The samples caught his interest because of their pharmaceutical significance. He wanted to know what animal contained the new "Mother Nature's natural brew."

"Well, this has all been very interesting, but I certainly haven't seen any monitors, big, small, or otherwise. I'll head back out to the ranch and have a look around. If you'll give me your name and number, I'll let you know if I come across anything else."

Mr. Cobb took Dr. Fletcher's information and thanked him for his time. He certainly did not want a team of biomedical researchers down here snooping around as well. Now what to do?

Chapter 15

# A New Season

The start of hunting season always breathed new life into Justice. The sleepy little town began to awaken with activity. Visitors began coming to town more regularly. The mercantile's huge stock of feeders and blinds for sale became permanent fixtures in the parking lot. Lines appeared at the gas pumps and the entrance to the restaurant. The new displays of camping equipment and camouflage that had gone up in August began to disappear.

It was exciting to see the influx of people. Besides the guides and trackers, who had been in town for a while, there were men from all walks of life—from professional athletes and their entourages, to doctors, lawyers, politicians, and businessmen. Few women made the hunting-weekend getaways. It was mostly a man's game, which was evident by the sale of beer and pork rinds.

The excitement bubbled over into the school. You could hear "Guess who I saw eating," "Guess who I saw buying chips at the mercantile," "Guess who is staying at our ranch," or "Guess who is going hunting with my dad," as each student tried to outdo the other. Even the teachers tried to cash in on the students' excitement by assigning essays with titles such as "What My Family Does on Opening Day." The atmosphere was almost carnival-like until Em's mother put her foot down.

"Are these people crazy? Have they forgotten guns can be quite violent? You children will not leave the house alone anymore. No more hiking or exploring trips unless your father and I are along."

Of course, that didn't stop Em and Marcus. Although Em had to persuade Marcus, he eventually realized that Mom wouldn't be home until after six, and if they were back by then, there would be no problem. Dad would be practicing with the basketball team at least that long, and during his season, he was much too serious to let the little kids play with his team. Em and Marcus were on their own, and it was much too boring to stay home. Plus, they were both anxious to see what Mr. Cobb's blind looked like and if he had done anything else at the site.

Em and Marcus were excited to get outside in the sun for a few hours after sitting in a classroom all day, but they weren't the only ones. As they approached the blind, they could hear voices. Usually, they did not want to get too close, for fear of leaving a scent or disturbing something, but today was different.

Em put a finger up to her lips and motioned for Marcus to stay down and be quiet. Em couldn't see much, but she recognized the voice. It was the same voice that ridiculed her when she fell off her bike—Justin! He wasn't alone either; he had a buddy along.

To her horror, they were adjusting the solar panels mounted on the blind as if they were deflecting laser beams from an unknown enemy. She couldn't control herself any longer. She burst out of the brush and announced, "You better cut that out! That's not yours. What do you think you are doing? You're trespassing!"

"So are you—this isn't your property, Miss Priss. You don't even belong here. Go away, and leave us alone. We ain't hurtin' nothin'."

"You'd better not because I know who all this stuff belongs to, and if any of it is broken or not working right, I'll make sure he knows to come looking for you!"

"Tattletale!" was all Justin could muster, and he jumped down, motioning for his compadre to follow. "We didn't hurt nothin'," he snorted again, "and you'll be sorry, Emeralda Ruiz!" They stormed past Em before they noticed Marcus still back in the brush. "Better mind your momma, boy," Justin jeered.

Marcus was mad, but he knew he was outnumbered. He approached Em undaunted, and Justin picked up the pace of his retreat. He kept a watchful eye on Marcus. He was a big kid, and a punch by surprise could do some damage.

"I'm sorry," Em said to Marcus. "I know I shouldn't have done that, but Mr. Cobb has worked hard on putting all this stuff together. I certainly don't want Justin messing it all up. Or worse, what if he found Pegasus? He would shoot it, stuff it, and mount it someplace!"

"Look, Em, we're not even sure what it was or if it is ever coming back. Picking fights we can't win won't help. I know you're mad, but if you had left Justin alone, he probably would have messed around for a while, become bored, and left. Now he'll come back just because he knows it will bother you."

Em frowned. She knew Marcus was probably right, but she still said, "We'll see." She never admitted defeat, but she knew this was a secret that needed protecting.

Chapter 16

# Science Fair

One good thing about school starting, from Em's perspective at least, was the assigning of projects. Em loved most school projects. It gave her the opportunity to be really creative. She was elated to go to the store and gather markers, paints, construction paper, and poster boards with which to showcase her work.

Science Fair came first, and she couldn't wait. She had had a great idea ever since she discovered the deer poop with Mr. Cobb. She decided to study how the decomposition of the little balls of poop affected fertilization. She had noticed some of the droppings seemed to last forever, and others seemed to dissolve into mounds of grass. Gross as it may seem, this project had a lot of potential. Based on her results, she might even be able to design a follow-up project that included environmental factors and what their roles might be in decomposition. Besides, all Science Fair judges liked to see projects that could be expanded by students with keen interests. Em certainly had a keen interest in this project.

Em had collected a bucketful of little, round deer droppings that she carefully divided into four batches. She had three identical flats. The first batch was her control. She did nothing except mix the droppings in potting soil, pour the mixture into the first flat, sprinkle it with grass seed, and water it. The next batch she mashed up with a shovel so that the droppings broke apart and were mixed more thoroughly into the potting soil. Then she continued planting as before. The third and fourth batches were her favorites. She painted and shellacked these to theoretically slow down or prevent their rate of decomposition. The third batch was mixed with potting soil and planted as before, but the fourth batch was given even more attention. These would be used to decorate her trifold. She painted and polished this last batch to resemble candy coated chocolate, and she was extremely pleased with the results.

All three flats were placed on their outdoor picnic table so that the sunlight and temperature would be the same for all. She watered them on a schedule, and her results were good. All three flats grew grass, and she was able to photograph and document the different stages and rates of growth for all three batches. Her data provided for excellent graphs.

Coach and Mrs. Ruiz were so proud of all the hard work Em had poured into this project. Mrs. Ruiz was happy to buy any paint or polish that Em needed as this project had kept her occupied and indoors.

On the final day of preparation, Em asked to go to the school early to set up. She surveyed the designated area in the cafeteria and picked out a prominent spot. She had written "Nature's Candy" at the top of her trifold, over the painted and polished droppings, and it could be seen from every spot in the cafeteria. Everything went perfectly, and now it was time for the final touch.

Justin had a younger brother named Martin. Although Em was no fan of Martin, she knew Justin wasn't either. In fact, Justin bullied poor Martin worst of all. She also knew Justin would know better than to accept a bag of candy from her, but would have no problem taking one away from his brother.

Em arranged to bump into Martin on his way to the cafeteria for breakfast that morning, at which time she secretly dropped a baggie of polished "candy" in his backpack and crossed her fingers.

"Oh," she said, "sorry, Martin. I didn't see you." She continued apologetically, "Guess I've got my mind on the Science Fair."

"Watch out, girl," Martin mumbled.

Em followed him into the cafeteria and watched as Martin got his breakfast and sat down with his backpack next to him on the bench. Just like clockwork, Justin entered with his thuggish friends. They popped Martin on the back of his head, poked his breakfast with their dirty fingers, and stole his cinnamon roll. But before they left, they delivered one final insult and knocked his backpack to the floor. Out fell the tempting bag of candy-coated "goodness." Em could not have scripted it any better.

"What have we here?" Justin asked.

"Those aren't mine," Martin whimpered.

"You're right; they're mine." Justin laughed. "C'mon, boys, let's go and have a snack," he sneered as they sauntered off with their loot. They walked to their spot and sat down.

Mr. Bigsby was standing in the corner with his coffee. Em timed it perfectly. All her Science Fair preparation was about to pay off. "Mr. Bigsby," she said, "one of my Science Fair bags is missing. Have you seen it? It had all my extra—"

Suddenly she was interrupted by a loud "AAAAAU-UUGH" followed by groaning, spitting, screaming girls, and then laughter, sweet laughter.

Justin jumped up, overturning a bench, and ran out of the cafeteria, moaning and wiping his tongue. Apparently, he had just poured a whole handful of what he thought was candy-coated M&M's into his mouth, chewed a couple of times, and spit them out, spraying pieces across the table.

"Those look like my decorations." Em acted astonished.

Mr. Bigsby looked over at her display and then back at her. "Is that what I think it is?" he asked.

"Deer droppings," she said matter-of-factly.

"You still want them back?"

"No, sir," she replied innocently. "They were extras from setup this morning. I just didn't want them to be mistaken for the real thing... Oh well." She turned and walked away. She should have won an Emmy.

"Oh well," repeated Mr. Bigsby under his breath as he motioned for one of the janitors.

Chapter 17

# The Shot

Mr. Cobb's finances were dwindling, as was his patience. He had been pursuing this animal actively for over a month. All his spare time was spent inspecting public lands, developing film, watching clips of video, and mapping his tracks. The videos had proved to be useless so far. The images were too grainy, and it was hard to distinguish shades of gray. The film was not much better. Although he did have a small collection of photos with unusual shadows on them, there was still nothing conclusive. He figured the surrounding country was already, or soon would be, dotted with feeders and blinds, so visiting his a little more often would not seem unusual. He was hoping to spend a few nights a week there just to see if he could spot anything his cameras couldn't.

Opening day came and went without any human fatalities at least. Mrs. Ruiz swore it was a miracle. She had made the children stay inside all day. A barrage of gunshots was heard all morning, as if they were watching a war movie on television. She got out all the old board games: Scrabble, Monopoly, and even Candyland. She made the time to play with them and was not leaving. She knew her children were way too curious about this new culture.

It sounded as if fireworks were exploding in the distance. The big, deep booms were so convincing that, more than once, Em found herself glancing up at the sky. The newness of it all would have killed Em if her mother had not kept her busy with all the games.

The following weekend, Mr. Cobb stopped by to visit. Everyone was glad to see him, especially Em. She could hardly wait to fill him in on all the trespassers' activities. Mr. Cobb explained that was the reason for his visit. His cameras had picked up some of the commotion, and he needed to check some of the equipment and readjust some of the camera placements. He asked if Em and Marcus would like to accompany him to the blind.

Although Mrs. Ruiz hesitated initially, she couldn't bear the thought of declining. Besides, it would be interesting to see where the kids had been exploring. She knew how important this little project was to them, and she knew Em would be mortified if she didn't allow them to tag along.

At their mother's request, Em and Marcus put on their old shoes and then ran ahead. Mr. Cobb had told them to stay quiet and wait for him outside the immediate area of the feeder so that it would remain undisturbed. He assured Mrs. Ruiz that he would enjoy their company and that they would not be in his way.

She smiled and waved, "Mind Mr. Cobb now, and remember we're following you."

On his family's place, Justin had not seen a single deer on opening day, and he remembered the feeder and blind Emeralda Ruiz had warned him about. He knew she was somehow responsible for his mouthful of deer poop, although he hadn't figured out how. He also knew that, in a heartbeat, she would tell on him about being in that blind, if she hadn't already. If he was going to get blamed for breaking something, he might as well hunt there at least once. Besides, if he shot a deer, he could always drag it to the back part of his family's fence line and claim it jumped over after it was shot, before it died. Not to mention, he was also curious and wanted to inspect all the gadgets he had played with last time. Maybe some of them could be used to track and target. Now that would be some high-tech hunting.

He got up right before sunrise and headed out. His parents would think he was in their blind, and Emeralda Ruiz would still be asleep, so no one would know.

Em and Marcus waited in the brush right before the clearing, just as Mr. Cobb had instructed. Em was standing impatiently, but Marcus crouched down to examine a footprint.

"Em," he whispered. "Look at this!"

As the sun crept higher and higher in the sky, Justin knew his chances of seeing a deer were dwindling. None of this fancy equipment had helped at all, not that he knew what any of it did. He just figured that someone else wouldn't have gone to all this trouble for nothing. Then, suddenly, he heard something. There was something causing the outskirts of the brush to move. Something was coming! Maybe this was the big one! He leveled his rifle and kept the scope focused on the brush.

Em bent over to get a closer look, but lost her balance and grabbed for Marcus's shoulder. Although she was able to catch her balance, Marcus fell sideways through the scrub.

He got up carefully and said, "Geez, Em, I hope we didn't scare anything away. Be careful!"

Just then, there was the familiar sound of a rifle firing, and Marcus felt a sharp sting. What? Instinctively he grabbed his shoulder. His shirt was turning bright red. "Em?"

Em's adrenaline took over. She knew it was a gunshot. Immediately she screamed, "Hold your fire! We're people!" She laid Marcus down and told him to keep his hand over the wound and keep pressing it down. Then she continued yelling, "Don't shoot," and barreled through the scrub brush, only to see panic-stricken Justin trying to make a quick getaway.

In his fear and haste to get away, Justin had caught his jeans on one end of the ladder. He finally tore them free when he saw Em.

"You idiot! What were you thinking? You shot my brother!"

"I'm sorry; I'm sorry—"

"You're sorry? You shot a person, stupid; I'm sorry doesn't cut it."

"Em," Marcus called.

"Marcus, be still. Be calm and don't get excited. Just try to stay calm, like Bert did after he was bit, remember?" She didn't know how bad Marcus's injury was. "Mr. Cobb and Mom are right behind us, and they'll know what to do. I'm sure Mr. Cobb has dealt with this kind of thing before, way out here in this country. You know he has a first aid kit and everything in the back of his truck. He'll know just what to do," she repeated.

"I-Is h-he g-going to d-die?" Justin stammered.

Em shot him a crazy look of disbelief. How could he even voice those words? Em looked Justin square in the eye. "No, Mr. Cobb is behind us," she repeated. Then her voice rose to a shout. "YOU go get Mr. Cobb NOW!" Her steely eyes showed no mercy. "You better not even think of trying to squirm your way out of this one. And RUN!!" she added.

Justin just stood there petrified.

Marcus knew Em was scared, and that frightened him. Em never got scared. He didn't want to cry. Big kids don't cry, but he couldn't help it. His eyes filled up and then just began to overflow.

"Like, NOW," Em screamed at Justin. "GO!" Then she returned to Marcus. "It'll be all right, Marcus. You'll see; it will be fine," she said reassuringly. But she couldn't help it; soon her eyes were overflowing too.

Suddenly they noticed another presence, and the Pegasus was there. He looked like an angry stallion reared on its hind legs. He was baring his teeth, and his ears were flattened, but Em was not afraid.

Justin didn't know exactly what he was seeing, but he was definitely not sticking around. If Emeralda was smart, she would find a way to grab Marcus and run too. No telling what that animal could do.

Once Justin had disappeared into the brush, the winged horse settled down. He was a little bigger than last time, but it was the same animal.

Em looked up at him. Tears were streaming down her face. "You're kidding... Could you pick a worse time?"

He nudged her aside gently to get to Marcus. Marcus did not look well at all. The Pegasus stood over him and nudged Marcus's hand away from the wound. Marcus was no longer strong enough to fight him off, so he allowed the Pegasus to lick the injury.

"No," Em cried. "We've got to keep pressure on it," she said as if the animal could understand. She reached to put her hands on the wound, but the horse pushed her away.

Marcus closed his eyes.

"No, no." Em began to sob. She was exhausted and surrendered to all her emotions as she tried to apply pressure to stop the bleeding. This was hopeless.

Mr. Cobb heard the shot, and so did Mrs. Ruiz. A cold shiver ran down his spine when he heard Emeralda yell, "Hold your fire!" He began an all-out sprint across the track and through the pasture. He could hear Mrs. Ruiz following. He knew she had to be feeling the same cold shiver or worse.

When he reached the clearing and saw Justin running towards him, he knew what happened. He should have seen this coming. He never should have let Em and Marcus go ahead. Mr. Cobb caught Justin by the shoulders, "How bad is it?"

Justin was still in shock and just stared blindly back at him.

Mr. Cobb shook him and repeated, "How bad?"

"He's b-b-bleeding," he stammered.

Mrs. Ruiz arrived just as Mr. Cobb released Justin, but she never even slowed down. Mr. Cobb called back to Justin as he followed Mrs. Ruiz, "You had better get the sheriff and have the ambulance waiting at their house when we get there." It was half order, half warning.

The closest 911 dispatch was fifty miles away, so the county had their own ambulance at the church for emergencies. Besides, Justin might need the sheriff to protect him once Coach Ruiz found out what happened, so he did what Mr. Cobb told him to do.

Mrs. Ruiz and Mr. Cobb ran stride for stride the rest of the way to the blind. When they got there, Mr. Cobb stopped dead in his tracks.

"Dear God," exclaimed Mrs. Ruiz.

Marcus was lying on the ground in a pool of blood, Em draped over him. Above him, a horse suddenly reared on its hind hooves, its magnificent wings outstretched and shimmering. The sun shone brightly behind it, making the spectacle appear heavenly.

Mr. Cobb held out his hand. "Easy, easy," he murmured.

The horse came back down on all fours and was clearly startled by Mrs. Ruiz's and Mr. Cobb's sudden presence. It began backing away.

"Mom," Em cried, "Justin shot him. I tried to keep pressure on it. Is he going to die? Mom, I don't want him to die. It was my fault. I fell and grabbed Marcus and—"

"It's okay, Em," Mrs. Ruiz broke in. She knelt next to her son. His breathing was slow, his pulse weak, but he was still alive. There was so much blood, but, at first glance, she couldn't find the wound. "Em, where did Marcus get shot? Do you know where?"

"His shoulder," Em answered and pointed.

Mrs. Ruiz found the hole in his shirt, front and back. His shirt was wet with warm blood, but there was no open wound. There was a fresh pink scar, one that hadn't been there before, just below his collarbone. It was circular, as if a blister had been peeled off before it dried all the way, but there was no blood coming out anywhere. She was puzzled. She stuck her fingers in the shirt's holes disbelievingly.

"How?" she asked.

Mr. Cobb forced himself to concentrate on the emergency at hand and not the wondrous beast. "The shot had to have gone straight through. We'll worry about how later, but for now we must get him to a hospital. He has lost a lot of blood." He gently picked up Marcus.

He turned to catch one more glimpse of the Pegasus before they left. Once again, no camera, no proof.

Chapter 18

# A Rescue

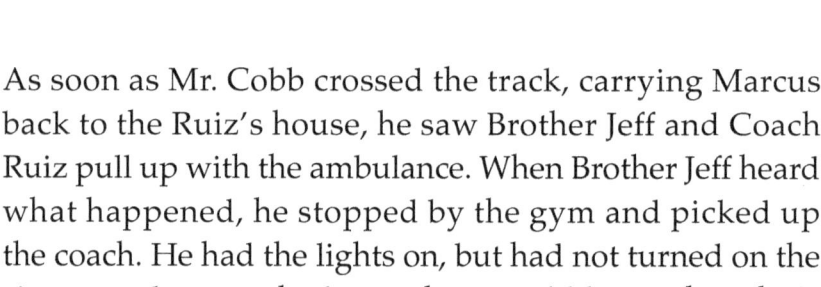

As soon as Mr. Cobb crossed the track, carrying Marcus back to the Ruiz's house, he saw Brother Jeff and Coach Ruiz pull up with the ambulance. When Brother Jeff heard what happened, he stopped by the gym and picked up the coach. He had the lights on, but had not turned on the sirens yet because he knew that would bring the whole town out and only create a traffic jam for him.

Mrs. Ruiz asked Mr. Cobb to stay with Em while she and Coach rode with Brother Jeff in the ambulance. As soon as Brother Jeff crossed the Frio River, right outside of town, he hit the sirens and floored the gas pedal of the old ambulance.

As soon as they were gone, Em turned to Mr. Cobb and asked, "What happened?"

"I'm not sure," he replied, "but let me say I believe you, Emeralda Ruiz. I think you did see a winged horse, and I just saw one too!"

They looked at each other incredulously and began to cry and laugh simultaneously. He put his arm around her reassuringly. "I'll tell you, though, there is NO way I would have believed it if I hadn't seen it. That was incredible!"

"Mr. Cobb, I saw Justin shoot Marcus. He was bleeding. I told Marcus to put pressure on it, and when he was too tired, I did." She looked at her bloodstained hands as if to make sure, and then she showed them to Mr. Cobb. She continued, "There was a hole in his shoulder. I felt his blood. It was warm. How did it stop? Did the Pegasus do that? Mom could not find the hole. How come?"

"I don't know, Em. I don't know," he repeated. There were a million things flashing through his brain like a music video: horse DNA, hollow bones for flight, feathers, healing saliva. How did the horse saliva heal? Wouldn't it have caused Marcus to bleed to death? Could this animal control his spit, or was it the "dust"? Everything was flooding his mind at once, and he couldn't organize his thoughts. There were so many pieces that needed to be put together to figure out this puzzle.

Em brought him back to reality. "What about Justin?" she asked.

That was the real kicker, wasn't it? How much had that kid seen and how much of it did he believe? It was possible that every hunter within a fifty-mile radius was loading up. That kid could never keep his mouth shut. But maybe he had left already. Maybe he had been so scared and in such a hurry to get Brother Jeff that he hadn't seen it. Could they really afford to gamble? If they were wrong, the Pegasus would be dead by morning.

"Em, we've got to go back and find it…find it before anyone else starts snooping around. It won't be good if word gets out. It will become a hunting prize."

Em was smart enough to know that. "But how do we find it? You've been looking all this time and haven't been able to find it."

"I'm not sure, Em. You're right. I haven't been able to find it, but you have twice. You tell me how you get it to come. Think, Em. How do you get it to come out?"

"I don't know." She sighed hopelessly. "The first time it was hurt, and we found it. The second time, Marcus was hurt, and it found us. Maybe it figured we saved his life, and now he saved ours—kind of a life debt repaid. Now that we are even, maybe he will never return."

"No, no, no. We've got to be missing something. It's been here all along. We just couldn't see it. Something happened that allowed us to see it. What was the same both times? Think."

Em closed her eyes and concentrated. She took a deep breath and blew it out. "Both times"—she concentrated—"both times it was Marcus and I."

"Okay, good," replied Mr. Cobb. "What else?"

Em thought. "Both times something was hurt."

Suddenly it hit her. She knew why it had come.

Mr. Cobb could see it on her face. "What, Em, what?!"

"I forgot. Bert was with us the first time too, and he got hurt. We were so scared we cried. Neither of us cries very often, but both times we cried. Do you think it heard us cry?"

"I think anything is possible at this moment, and I think you are our best chance. Here's what I need you to do."

Chapter 19

# A Plan

By the time they arrived at the hospital, nearly an hour later, the physician couldn't explain Marcus's injury. He said there was no way a gunshot could have inflicted such an injury. Although Marcus was severely dehydrated, he wasn't convinced the blood on his shirt was his. Sometimes in cases of severe dehydration, hallucination can occur. Perhaps, the doctor postulated, a gun was shot nearby, or maybe even an animal was shot, and Marcus found it.

Fortunately for all involved, Em did not get to talk to the doctor because there was no way she would have settled for such a story. Although Mrs. Ruiz had not actually seen what happened, she witnessed enough to know that her son had not been hallucinating. However, she also knew that neither she nor anyone else in their party wanted to draw attention to such an extraordinary event until they themselves had a chance to figure it out.

The doctor said he would check on Marcus again after his IV. Barring any unforeseen complications, Marcus would be able to go home that evening.

Mr. and Mrs. Ruiz breathed a sigh of relief.

Em went into the brush alone. She still had tears in her eyes, more from worry than from fear. She was worried about Marcus. Had the winged horse really healed him? Was it even possible, or was she dreaming it all? What about Justin? What would he do? What had he seen?

She found the spot Marcus had been shot. His blood was still wet on the ground. She knelt and touched it. It was still warm. She knew it came out of her brother, and bad things happen when someone loses a lot of blood.

She began to cry. Marcus had to be all right. He was the one who always backed her up and defended her honor. He made sure no one took advantage of her or treated her with less respect than she deserved. He was her brother. And now…now…he wasn't even here. She felt so alone. How could she find this animal without him?

Suddenly she knew it had found her.

It approached cautiously, and Em froze like a statue. It sniffed the blood, raised its head, and whinnied its disapproval. It reared on its hind legs and spread its magnificent wings. The fairy dust sprinkled down around her as if she had entered Neverland.

For a second, it was surreal, but she realized the winged horse thought she was the one hurt now. "No, no," she whispered, "I'm not hurt."

She softly touched its wings and brought them down. She gently petted its nose, and it nuzzled her neck. What an incredible creature.

Then she heard a four-wheeler in the distance, and she knew trouble was on its way. She remembered what Mr. Cobb had told her. Full of awe, fear, and dread, she coaxed the animal to come with her.

Mr. Cobb had a plan, a far-fetched, crazy one, but still a plan. He knew Em's best chances of finding the winged horse were if she was alone. From what he had witnessed, the animal appeared to be the furthest thing from a threat, especially to the children.

He quickly took his truck to the school and hitched up the agriculture class's stock trailer. It was covered with long slats along the sides. The slats could be maneuvered to serve as blinds to help keep the animals from getting spooked, especially when traveling. The trailer could hold several horses, but he only needed it to hold one.

He was on good terms with the agriculture teacher and had borrowed it on several occasions. Certainly no one would think it strange that he had borrowed it again. Besides, he would hopefully be able to return it before anyone missed it.

After he attached the trailer to his truck, he drove back behind the Ruiz's house and kept his fingers crossed, his eyes searching the brush just beyond the track. Minutes later, Em appeared out of the scrub brush, coaxing a horse along, by her side. It looked like the animal he had seen earlier, but his wings were virtually indistinguishable against his body. It was amazing.

Mr. Cobb held a blanket in his hands. The creature stammered a bit at the sight of him and the trailer, but Em was reassuring.

Tears were flowing freely from her cheeks as she sensed the impending danger. The four-wheeler sound was getting closer, and although it was not yet visible, in the distance she could make out whooping, hollering, and other masculine frivolity that often accompanied boys. The animal, perhaps, sensed her fear, as it did her pain, and became more docile.

Mr. Cobb led it into the trailer, draped a blanket over its back, and said, "It'll be all right. I promise."

Em couldn't tell if he was speaking to her or the winged horse, and her eyes continued to water as she waved goodbye. There was no time to waste, though. She wiped her face dry with the backs of her hands.

Em followed Mr. Cobb's instructions to a tee. She grabbed her bike and headed to the sheriff's office. Just as Mr. Cobb had predicted, the sheriff was heading to her house, so Em had to distract him long enough for Mr. Cobb to make a quick stop and then get out on the main road and out of Justice.

It wasn't hard. Em gave her view of Justin's reckless, cowardly shooting. She went on to say that she thought he had told his cousins and that they were on their way to get her because she was the only witness. She could hear the four-wheelers, loud laughter, and hollering. Her parents weren't back from the hospital yet, and she was scared.

The sheriff was astonished. "Where's Cobb?" he asked.

"He got a call and had to leave. Something about some hunters cutting some rancher's fence...after some deer, I think." Em could be a masterful liar, especially when the stakes were high, and they didn't get any higher in her book.

"What in the heck is going on?" the sheriff asked rhetorically.

He put out an all-points bulletin for Mr. Cobb's truck. He knew Mr. Cobb well enough to know that if he ran across a mad horse, as Justin had suggested to him earlier, he would do everything he could to protect the animal before it was destroyed. He had not bought into the whole wing thing that the kid had described, but he knew he had to get to the bottom of this. A mad horse could do a lot of damage and cause serious injury. Now little Miss Ruiz had a different story about Justin accidentally shooting at her brother, not at a mad horse, which sounded more believable, knowing Justin.

Em began to get worried, but then the sheriff told her to go home and wait for her parents; he would take care of everything. He sped off, spitting gravel from his rear wheels, and headed toward the back end of the track, toward Justin's family's land, planning to corner any rowdies before anything else happened.

Crazy stories from kids about winged horses, a mystery shooting, overzealous hunters—the sheriff was afraid to ask what else could happen. Was there a full moon? It wasn't even Saturday night yet! He hoped Mr. Cobb would surface so he could shed some light on what really happened. He had heard Em's side of the story; now he needed to revisit with Justin and, perhaps, break something up before it got worse. As soon as he had that under control, he was going to have to check on Marcus. He was still not quite sure if he had been shot or bit, or what. He couldn't get anything out of the hospital, other than he was alive.

## Chapter 20
# An Escape

Mr. Cobb drove as fast as he could pull a trailer. He was on the main road heading south-southwest toward Mexico. It was the logical choice for those seeking to evade questioning by US officials, but was he really evading officials? How far was he willing to go to protect this secret creature? Was he breaking any laws? He didn't have time to think it through. He was quickly approaching the Kanter County line, heading toward the town of Angelina, although he had no intention of reaching it.

Mr. Cobb didn't see the dark vehicle approaching from his rear, but when the lights came on, he knew his journey was over. "Well, that didn't take long," he said under his breath and hoped everything was still okay.

The officer approached cautiously and asked for his license and registration. Nothing looked out of the ordinary to the officer, and he wondered what this was about. He asked where Mr. Cobb was headed in such a hurry away from town, with a trailer no less.

Mr. Cobb said he had been called out because of a cut fence, and he grabbed the trailer in case some livestock had made it to the road, causing problems. Fortunately, none had, and he was now headed to Angelina to get some gas before heading back. Gas was always a little cheaper in Angelina.

The officer glanced at Mr. Cobb's gas gauge. It read a quarter of a tank, which would indeed be low, considering how far apart the gas stations were.

Mr. Cobb asked the officer if there was a problem.

The officer made no reply, but told Mr. Cobb to sit tight, and he headed back to his patrol car to radio his findings. The officer was surprised when dispatch replied the Kanter County sheriff himself wanted the trailer searched for any animals. That seemed like a strange request, especially since he could see through the slats that the trailer was empty, but he had been asked to do stranger things.

He got back out of his vehicle and approached Mr. Cobb. He explained he had orders to check the contents of his trailer unless Mr. Cobb objected.

"Heck no, I don't mind, sir. You can see it's empty." Mr. Cobb got out of the vehicle and opened the back of the trailer. Indeed, it was empty, except for a bit of hay blowing around on the floor. "I don't mean any disrespect, but are you sure you got the right truck?"

The officer was wondering the same thing. After a brief conversation with dispatch, he unhappily informed Mr. Cobb he was to escort him back to Justice.

Neither was thrilled at the prospect. "Can you make it there towing this trailer on a quarter of a tank?" the officer asked.

"Guess I'll have to," Mr. Cobb replied, and they headed back.

The sheriff was a waiting for Mr. Cobb in his office and thanked the trooper for escorting him back before dismissing the officer. After questioning Mr. Cobb, and with no winged horse, no animal of any kind, and a story that sounded an awful lot like Emeralda Ruiz's, the sheriff was totally frustrated. What was that little dope Justin up to? Whatever it was, it would have to wait until tomorrow. His stomach had been telling him for the past hour that it was way past suppertime.

Chapter 21

# Onward

Marcus was still weak after the IV, so the doctor wanted to keep him in the hospital twenty-four hours for observation. Mrs. Ruiz was not about to leave, so Coach Ruiz rode back with Brother Jeff in the ambulance.

It was late when they reached Justice. Coach thanked Brother Jeff for all he had done—getting the ambulance, staying with them, and driving him home. He also thanked him for all the prayers, which was totally out of character for him. However, he too had been shaken by the day's events.

Coach Ruiz planned to pick up Em and head back to the hospital, at least for a little while. He knew Em would want to see her brother, and that would be one way to make sure she didn't get into any more trouble.

Brother Jeff waited for Coach Ruiz to get inside his house, and then he slowly backed the ambulance out of the driveway and turned on his headlights. It was beginning to get dark, and he was anxious to get back to the church. He was worn out after all the excitement.

The gravel crunched under the ambulance's tires as Brother Jeff turned off the road and onto the dirt drive that led to the little shed that housed the ambulance. He got out of the ambulance, pulled up the shed's door to drive inside, and got a big surprise.

There stood a horse with a blanket across its back. There was a note pinned to it.

*Brother Jeff,*

*Please house my horse for a little while.*
*It is very special and needs sanctuary.*
*I'll come for him as soon as I can.*

*Thanks,*
*Clayton*

Brother Jeff returned to the ambulance and pulled the keys from the ignition. Best to leave the ambulance out tonight, he figured.

Just as Brother Jeff turned, Mr. Cobb drove up in his truck. He had just returned the trailer to the school. He parked next to the ambulance.

"Well, that certainly wasn't long at all," Brother Jeff said. "How are you doing, Clay? It's been quite a day, I hear."

"Brother," Mr. Cobb looked him straight in the eye and said, "I've seen things today that I don't know what to make of." He paused for a moment and then added, "But I do know I can trust you, or I wouldn't have come, and

I certainly wouldn't have brought this horse." Their eyes were now locked. "I have one more favor to ask of you."

"Of course. You know I'll do anything that doesn't break the law," Brother Jeff replied.

Mr. Cobb smiled briefly. "No, sir. No laws being broken. I just need to borrow your ambulance—for my horse, that is."

Brother Jeff looked at the horse. It certainly was a beautiful creature. It didn't appear to be hurt. He looked back at Mr. Cobb. "Godspeed" was all he said, and he placed the keys in the palm of Mr. Cobb's hand.

Mr. Cobb laid his other hand on top Brother Jeff's, held him for a moment, and then repeated, "Yes, sir, Godspeed."

As soon as Mr. Cobb reached the open road, he turned on the ambulance's red and blue lights and bore down on the accelerator. No stopping now. He was headed northwest to the open country. Rugged land, free skies, and few people—that is what they needed. With a little more assistance, maybe he could help preserve this magnificent species a little longer. Godspeed indeed.